I0763407

The Christmas Cookie

Stories from the Counter

By David Gregory

The Christmas Cookie

ISBN: 979-8-9999902-1-1

Cover design by [David Gregory/AI-assisted design]

Printed in the United States of America

For those who've ever found clarity in a quiet moment and comfort in a warm cookie.

"The cookie doesn't change you.

It shows you."

- *Karen*

Welcome to the Shoppe

The bell above the door always chimes the same way — soft, warm, almost like it knows you're coming. Snow may fall heavier some days than others, but in here, there's always a chair waiting, the air rich with coffee and quiet company.

On the counter, beneath the glass dome, rests *The Christmas Cookie.* Ordinary to the eye. Extraordinary to the soul. It doesn't grant wishes or offer easy answers. It simply reveals — showing what waits beneath the surface, what you most need to see.

People rarely come looking for magic. They come for coffee, or a pause in their day, or sometimes just a bit of warmth against the cold. But almost everyone leaves with more than they expected. Some walk out lighter. Some heavier. None unchanged.

These stories are gathered moments. Each is its own journey — a glimpse into the quiet turning point of another soul. You don't need to read them in order. Open anywhere, and you'll find yourself in the middle of someone's moment of seeing, of shifting, of becoming.

The cookie is always there. The journey is always yours.

So, welcome. Sit down. The snow can wait.

Prologue

Some recipes are meant to be found, not made

In the heart of Brookhaven Pines,
Gregory keeps *The Bake Shoppe* —
a cozy haven known for its rich coffee,
its decadent cookies,
and a mysterious warmth people can't quite explain.

Outside snow may drift and swirl,
but inside, the bell above the door
always chimes the same familiar note —
a reminder that every story begins somewhere

On the far corner of the glass case rests The Christmas Cookie —
an unassuming sugar cookie
with a delicate golden shimmer.

It's never sold.
Sometimes offered.
Sometimes requested.
Always a choice.

One quiet evening,
I was reorganizing the counter — half working, half avoiding a stack of receipts I didn't want to face.

That's when I found it.

The recipe.

Tucked into the back of an old leather notebook,
its cover softened by time,
its pages frayed at the edges.

In the center: a folded sheet of yellowed paper,
the handwriting instantly familiar —
Karen's elegant loops and steady hand.

The Christmas Cookie.
The name underlined twice.

A list of ingredients simple enough,
yet heavy with something older.
Something meant to be found.

I don't know what possessed me —
maybe the cloves on the shelf behind me,
maybe the way the street outside seemed to hold its breath.

But I gathered the ingredients
and began to bake.

An hour later, they cooled on the rack.
I poured coffee,
lifted one still-warm cookie,
and took a bite.

The shop faded.

Heat.
Sunlight.
A voice I hadn't heard in decades — my own, younger.

I was back in a moment I'd long since buried,
one tangled with choices I hadn't wanted to own.

And there it was.
Waiting.

When I blinked, I was back in the shop.
Coffee still hot.
Half-eaten cookie on the plate.

And then the door opened.

Karen stepped inside, brushing snow from her coat,
her eyes twinkling like she'd just heard the best secret in the world.

"Morning, Gregory," she said.
"Pour me a cup of your amazing coffee…
and one of those Christmas cookies."

We locked eyes.
She knew.
I knew.
And she knew that I knew.

"How was your journey?" she asked softly.

I smiled.
"Let's just say…
I understand what the recipe was really about."

The Morning Walk

Greetings, cherished recipes, and a promise beneath the glass

From the living room of my 1950's renovated bungalow,
I could hear the muffled scrape of shovels,
the hiss of snow brushed from awnings,
the steady rhythm of a town waking up.
The first breath outside was always sharp with winter's metallic edge —
but it woke me like nothing else.

Evergreen Street had been my dream long before I lived here —
a walk to work that wasn't just a commute,
but a string of familiar faces.

I'd watched my parents
build that kind of community when I was a kid:
neighbors, shopkeepers, church friends —
connections that lasted decades.

I wanted that for myself.

Mrs. Donnelly from the flower shop was unlocking her door.
"Morning, Gregory! Tell Karen I said hello!"

Two doors down, Tom was walking Bailey, his golden retriever,
a paper bag from the diner swinging in his hand.
"Save me a table by the window," he called.

At Peter's place, he stood out front with a coffee,
looking like someone replaying a conversation he wished had gone differently.

"Morning," I said.

He groaned.
"Another four-week masterpiece down the drain.
Starting to think I'm cursed."

Peter was smart, funny, handsome,
and could charm his way through most situations —
except, apparently, love.

Over the years we'd shared more than a few afternoons
dissecting his latest crash-and-burn.

I wasn't sure what role he'd play in *this* season's story,
but I had a feeling he'd be back.

By the time I reached The Bake Shoppe,
the air inside wrapped around me in cinnamon,
espresso,
and butter warming in the ovens.

This shop — my shop —
had started as a dream in my mother's kitchen,
the youngest of six kids breathing in the smells of chocolate chip,
icebox,
minty jewel,
fudge,
bon bons,
and her infamous bishop's bread —
her sly, delicious rebuttal to fruitcake.

She never called the people who came through our front door
"customers."
They were guests.

That's how I see them still —
not transactions, but moments of connection.

Guests enrich you in ways you can't predict.
Always better than you thought it would be.

I unlocked the front door.
Embers glowed faintly in the corner fireplace.

In an hour, the shop would be alive —
cups clinking,
Nat King Cole on the stereo,
ovens humming in the back.

And this year…
there was something new.

Something waiting under glass on the back shelf,
something Karen had a hand in,
whether she'd ever admit it or not.

The Christmas Cookie.

But that, as my mother would say,
was a story worth savoring.

For the Journey

Origins, Choices, and Invitations

The air was alive with the steady hum of the coffee grinder,
the hiss of steamed milk,
the crackle of the fireplace.
The scent was intoxicating —
espresso, cinnamon, butter,
and something deeper.

A fresh batch of cookies cooled on the counter,
steam curling faintly upward.
They weren't just any cookies.
They were *the* cookies.

The recipe had been tucked between the pages of an old cookbook in the back room — the one filled with my mother's recipes I'd long since memorized.

I knew the handwriting at once: Karen.
My oldest friend.
My mirror.
My truth-teller for nearly three decades.

At the very bottom, in the margin,
she'd written three small words:

**For the journey.**

Karen wasn't just a friend.
She was stitched into the fabric of my life.
The woman who could tilt her head,
catch your silence,
and suddenly make you feel seen.

Karen never did anything without reason.
Which is why I didn't think finding that recipe was an accident.

I made the first batch out of curiosity.
Butter. Sugar. Flour.

…And one ingredient I'd never seen in a cookie before.
(That one's between me and the recipe.)

I poured myself a latte,
set one on a plate,
and took a bite.

The first taste was everything you'd expect —
soft, rich, spiced like Christmas
without tipping into cliché.

But halfway through, something shifted.
The air thickened.
The sound of the grinder faded.

My heart picked up —
not from caffeine,
but from being pulled somewhere else.

I opened my eyes,
and I wasn't in the shop anymore.

I was standing on a quiet street I knew from years ago —
the one from that day.
The one I never talk about.
The one where,
if I'd only been more aware,
more responsible,
I might have avoided everything that came after.

Only now…
it wasn't memory.
It was happening again.

The conversation.
The expression on their face.
The choice I'd made without thinking.

Frame by frame,
I felt the weight of it —
the sting of what I caused,
and the possibility of what I could have done differently.

Then — just as suddenly —
I was back in the shop.

Latte still hot.
Half a cookie on the plate.

The door jingled.

Karen stepped inside, scarf dusted with snow.
She slipped into her favorite seat by the window,
loosening her scarf with the practiced grace of someone
who had long ago made peace with exactly who she was.

She placed her leather gloves neatly on the table,
then looked up at me.

"You've made the cookie, I see."

I didn't ask how she knew.
"Maybe," I said, smiling back with mischief.

Her eyes softened into that knowing smile.
"Well then," she said, voice warm but edged with play,
"how was your journey?"

We locked eyes in that moment.
I didn't answer.

"Gregory," she said, voice warm but lined with mischief.
"Two things: one, my usual coffee — extra hot, you know how I like it.
And two…"

Her eyes flicked toward the cooling rack.
"One of those."

I delivered her coffee, she lifted her cup, sipping slowly,
the December light framing her in that timeless way
photographs try to capture but rarely do.

She looked at me, still holding the cookie, and smiled.
Not her polite smile. Her knowing one.
I just gestured toward the plate I had set down before her.
She adjusted in her chair,
her grin widening.

"Oh, Greg," she said softly.
"You have no idea where that one might take me."

That wasn't the first time Karen and the cookie crossed paths.
Not by a long shot.

As she leaned back in her chair,
her eyes steady on the golden cookie cooling between us.

She traced the rim of her mug, as if weighing whether to let me in on something she'd carried for decades

"I never told you the first time I had one," she said,
her voice low enough that only I could hear.

It was 1968.
She was seventeen.

Restless.
Certain the world wasn't going to hand her anything.

A neighbor — an old woman with a quiet smile
and a kitchen cluttered with mixing bowls,
lace curtains,
and the faint smell of nutmeg —
had offered her a single cookie on Christmas Eve.

Karen took a bite
and suddenly stood in her parents' living room, three years earlier.

She watched her younger self refuse a chance to leave home for a scholarship.

In that moment, she saw it clearly:
the fear in her own eyes —
fear dressed up as practicality.

"When I came back," Karen said,
"I realized I'd been carrying that moment like a locked box.

The cookie didn't change the past, Gregory —
it changed my relationship to it.

That's what makes it magic.

You get to see yourself without the excuses."

And yet, as powerful as that first taste had been,
Karen still carried other moments, other choices,
tucked away like folded letters.

In the glow of the late afternoon, the shop was illuminated once again with that holiday light that softened the edges of everything it touched.

Outside, snowflakes drifted lazily past the window,
catching in the lamplight like tiny sparks.

Karen lingered at her table, the golden cookie still fresh but waiting. She smiled knowingly, reminding me this wasn't about caffeine and dessert.

She picked it up, studied it for a moment, and then took a deliberate bite.

Her eyes closed a beat too long,
her breathing shifting as though she'd just remembered a scent from childhood.

Her smile softened into something almost wistful.

I've seen a lot in this shop —
first dates,
breakups,
family reconciliations,
reunions that turned strangers back into friends.

But this moment was different.

It was as if she'd stepped out of herself without leaving the table.

I wanted to ask what she was seeing.
But I knew better. Minutes passed.
Finally, her focus returned.
She set the cookie down as though it were made of glass.

"Gregory," she said softly, "that was twenty years ago.
I thought I'd put it away."

"What happened?" I asked gently.

She shook her head and smiled — the smile that says, not yet.

"Let's just say," she murmured, wrapping her hands around her mug,
"I was given a choice that day.

Now I see the choice I could have made."

Her eyes met mine, but she didn't need to explain further.

I knew the way that cookie worked.
It didn't just show the past;
it brought you to the edge of responsibility.

Whether you stepped over…
well, that was up to you.

That was Karen — never treating the cookie like an answer,
but always like an invitation.

And in time, she became the quiet witness to others taking their first step.

She sipped her coffee, and then — as if nothing extraordinary had just happened — asked, "So, how's business?"

And So It Begins

The First Customer of the day

The door chimed,
letting in a swirl of cold air
and the faint scent of pine from the wreath outside.

Overhead, a soft instrumental of *Have Yourself a Merry Little Christmas*
drifted through the stereo,
mingling with the hiss and sigh of the espresso machine.

She stepped in — mid-thirties,
hair damp from melting snow,
cheeks pink from the wind.

A leather tote hung from one arm;
a phone clutched in the other like a lifeline.

She ordered a latte,
her voice polite but far away —
as though she'd left most of herself somewhere else.

Then her eyes shifted to the pastry case,
scanning gingerbread,
shortbread,
sugar-dusted crescents —
until they stopped.

She leaned in, lowering her voice.
"Do you… have *The Christmas Cookie*?"

From her corner table, Karen looked up from her book.
She didn't speak,
but her lips curved in the faintest knowing smile.

I stepped to the back shelf
and lifted the small, covered cake stand.

One cookie rested there, golden and unassuming,
its sugar catching the light.
She smiled faintly.
"I guess that one's mine."

I smiled back.
"Seems it was meant for you."

She hesitated.
"Is it true? About… the experience?"

I leaned in,
my voice nearly lost under the hum of the shop.
"That's for you to find out."

I slid the plate toward her,
the warmth wafting upward in a swirl of cinnamon,
nutmeg,
and something else —
something you couldn't quite name.

She carried it to a table in the corner,
brushed a strand of hair behind her ear,
and broke the cookie in half.

Her first bite was cautious —
but in an instant her gaze unfocused,
her shoulders dropped,
and even the Christmas music seemed to hush,
as though the world had stepped back
to let her go where she needed to.

When she returned — whenever that truly was —
her smile shimmered with tears.

"Thank you," she whispered,
leaving the other half untouched.

Then she slipped into the falling snow,
latte in hand,
the bell above the door chiming her departure.

Karen closed her book with slow deliberation,
still smiling.
“And so it begins — as it always does.”

The Soldier's Story

A Memory in Uniform

The bell over the door rang sharp against the hush,
letting in a gust of December air
and a young man in uniform.

Snow clung to his boots.
His shoulders carried a weight far heavier than the pack on his back.

He ordered only coffee — black —
and settled by the window,
where the glass quivered with the storm outside.

His gaze stayed fixed on the street,
but his fingers betrayed him.

Restless.
Tapping.
Clenching.
Opening again —
as though fighting a battle no one else could see.

Karen noticed.
She always noticed.

She carried her cup across the room and sat nearby,
her voice light but sure.

"Gregory sometimes has sweets that aren't on the menu."

The young man looked up, puzzled.
She only tilted her head toward the counter.

I lifted the glass dome,
and the cookie waited — unassuming, patient.

He almost laughed. "That's it?" A cookie?"

Karen gave him that look,
the one that silences doubt without a word.

I delivered it to his table.
He broke the cookie in half,
studied it like it might dissolve if he breathed too hard,
then took a bite.
His eyes shut.

A breath left his chest in a slow, shaking exhale.

He swallowed once, twice,
then pressed the heel of his hand against his eyes.

"It's… her recipe.
My mom's.
She baked these every Christmas morning."

The word mom splintered in his throat.

His laugh was half-sob, half-wonder.
"I haven't tasted this since—"

His voice collapsed under the weight of what he couldn't say.

Karen reached across and touched his hand.
Gentle. Certain.
"Then you've come to the right place."

He finished quietly.
Stood, nodded to me —
a soldier's thank-you.

Then he left.

The Elder Couple

Perhaps Today

They entered slowly,
a gentleness that comes from years of walking side by side.

Heavy coats. Gloves tucked away.
Eyes that scanned the room until they found their corner —
their place.

I was already pouring their tea before they asked.
Old friends don't need words for such things.

She leaned on his arm as they settled,
her voice barely above a breath.

"Perhaps today."

He nodded, rose,
and crossed to the counter
with the dignity of a man still a little shy in love.

"Would there be… a *Christmas Cookie*?"

I set the plate before them.
One cookie, unbroken until they broke it together.

Half each.
Slow bites.
Quiet smiles.

A language older than words,
spoken only between them.

They first met at a Christmas-season military dance,
uniforms, hope, borrowed time.

He asked her for a single song.
And before it ended, he asked her for forever.

They'd been dancing together ever since —
every December, every Christmas,
and now every cookie they shared side by side.

Whenever he reached for her hand, he still hummed that holiday refrain
from the night they first danced…
carried across decades of devotion …and love.

From across the room, Karen felt the shop still itself —
floorboards holding their creak,
the kettle quieting its hiss —
as though time bent respectfully
around the couple's ritual.

When the last crumb was gone,
they stayed a while longer,
their hands folded together on the table.

Then they rose,
side by side,
and left as they had come.

The door closed gently,
like a blessing.

The Young Man with the Shaky Hands

What You Choose to Hold Onto

The shop had settled into a gentle lull —
Christmas music faded into the background.
Outside, the first flurries of snow
danced past the window.

I was wiping down the counter
when the bell above the door gave its shy chime.
He slipped in like someone who didn't want to be seen.
Hoodie up.
Shoulders hunched.
Hands jammed deep into his pockets.
When he finally set them on the counter,
I noticed the faint tremor.
Not overwhelming,
but steady enough to catch the eye.

He ordered a coffee without looking at me,
his voice barely above the music.

Avoiding eye contact, he hesitated
before asking if *"the special"* was still available.

I gently smiled and nodded.
"Always."

I set the cookie down with his coffee.

He didn't touch it right away —
just stared at it,
as though afraid of what it might reveal.

Finally, he broke it in half
and ate a piece.

The shop faded.

His eyes unfocused.

He was carried back to age fourteen —
standing in a school hallway outside the auditorium,
too afraid to step inside.

The spring play auditions were underway,
and he wanted to try out so badly
he could feel it in his ribs.

But fear chained him there,
whispering that avoiding humiliation
was safer than risking it.

Only this time, he moved.

He opened the door.
He walked to the stage.

When his turn came, the words shook,
but he spoke them anyway.

The room erupted in applause.

A warm hand landed on his shoulder.

The drama teacher's voice was soft but certain:
"Showing up is the bravest thing you'll ever do."

He blinked — and the shop was back.
His coffee sat untouched.

He wiped at his eyes, breathless.
"It was just one little thing," he murmured.
He looked up at me. "But it changes everything, doesn't it?"

I smiled.
"It can, if you want it to."

He glanced at his hands, still resting on the cup.
The tremor hadn't vanished,
but it had softened — quieter now, almost unfamiliar.
And for the first time,
he realized what we choose to hold onto
can steady us — in body, mind, spirit.

"Will my hands ever stop shaking?" he asked with emotion.

"The question isn't whether your hands will ever stop shaking,"
Karen said quietly.
"It's what you choose to hold onto when they do."

He left the other half of the cookie on the plate
and walked out into the snow,
the corners of his mouth lifting
like he'd just remembered how.

The Man Who Walked Out

The Door That Stayed Open

The afternoon carried a restless edge.
The wind rattled the wreath on the front door,
and snow came in quick bursts —
not the peaceful postcard kind,
but the kind that made people hunch their shoulders and hurry.
Inside, the fire glowed,
the shop warm and golden against the gray outside.

Karen was at her usual table,
crossword puzzle angled just so,
pen moving at its unhurried pace.

The bell above the door jingled,
and a man in his late fifties stepped in.

Neatly dressed — not flashy,
but deliberate.

His eyes scanned the room
before fixing on me behind the counter.

"Coffee. Black."

I poured it, slid it across.

He handed me exact change
without breaking eye contact.

Then his gaze shifted
to the small glass stand at the back.

"That the famous cookie?"

His tone was somewhere between curiosity and challenge.

"Some call it that," I said with a small smile.

He smirked.
"So, what's the gimmick?

People eat it, cry a little,
and walk out thinking life's fixed?"

Karen's pen paused mid-word.
She didn't look up,
but I knew she was listening.

I lifted the dome,
placed a single cookie on a plate,
and set it in front of him.

"No gimmick.
Just an invitation.
A choice."

He stared at it for a moment,
then gave a short laugh.

"I've made it sixty years
without needing some sugar-coated therapy session.
I think I'm good."

"It only works if you want to see something,"
I said evenly.

He pushed the plate back toward me.
"And what if I'm fine not seeing?"

Karen finally looked up,
her eyes steady on him.

"Then you'll stay exactly where you are," she said softly.

His jaw tightened.
He straightened his coat.

"Maybe that's the point.
Some of us don't need… whatever this is."

Without another word,
he turned and walked out,
the bell above the door giving a sharper chime than usual.

I looked over at Karen with a mischievous smile
I would give her once in a while
when we both knew what was coming.

"You knew he wouldn't take it."

She went back to her puzzle.
"I knew he couldn't.
There's a difference."

I set the untouched cookie back under the dome.
"Do you think he'll be back?"

Karen's smile was faint, almost wistful.
"Everyone comes back eventually.

The question is whether there's still time when they do."

The Woman Who's Always in Control

Letting Go of Control Isn't the Same as Losing Control

The shop was steady that morning.
Not rushed.
Not slow.
Just the kind of rhythm where you could hear
the espresso machine hum like a heartbeat.

The bell above the door rang,
and she entered like she owned the room.

Perfect posture.
Designer coat buttoned all the way.
Every hair pinned into place.

She scanned the shop with quick efficiency,
her gaze weighing and measuring
before she approached the counter.

"Latte. Extra hot. One pump vanilla. No foam."

The order came out like an instruction, not a request.

I nodded, started preparing it.

"And I suppose," she added,
eyes narrowing toward the glass stand,
"that's the cookie I've heard about?"

"Yes," I said simply.

She leaned in, voice low.
"How does it work?
What exactly… happens?" with a shrug of her shoulders.

I smiled.
"That depends.
Every experience is different."

Her lips pressed into a line.
"I don't like surprises.
Tell me what to expect."

Before I could answer,
Karen's voice floated from her table
without looking up from her crossword:
"That's not how it works."

The woman bristled.
"So it's random?"

"Not random," I said, sliding her latte across.
"Just… honest."

I lifted the dome
and placed a cookie on a plate.

She hesitated, then squared her shoulders
and broke off a piece
as if bracing for battle.

She chewed, her expression neutral —
until her hand trembled slightly
as she set the cup down.

The shop faded.

She was twelve,
standing in the middle of a family dinner
where her parents' argument had flared into chaos.

Voices sharp, plates rattling.
Her younger brother cried into his mashed potatoes.

And she — the only one steady enough to take charge —
stood up, told everyone to stop,
and carried her brother out of the room.

She'd never stopped taking charge after that.
Not once.
Not with friends.
Not at work.
Not even with herself.

Always steady.
Always the rescuer.
Always the one who controlled.

But in that memory,
as she sat on the hallway floor
with her brother's small head against her shoulder,
she realized her hands had been shaking the whole time.

The shop returned.

She gripped the counter like it was an anchor.
"I… I don't let go. Ever." her brow furrowed at the epiphany.

Karen's pen paused mid-word.
Her voice was soft, certain.

"Control isn't strength.
It's resistance to responsibility."

The woman swallowed hard,
lifted her latte,
and straightened her coat.

"I'll… keep that in mind."

She left the cookie half-eaten,
walked out with her chin still high —
but her steps were slower,
her heels not quite as sharp against the floor.

Not Much of a Sweets Person

Don't Wait Until Silence Has the Last Word

Karen was at her table —
not with her book or crossword,
but with a small tin of star-shaped cookies she'd brought in.
She was handing them out to anyone who ordered a drink,
weaving little stories with each one —
where the recipe came from,
who used to make them,
why the points of the star mattered.

The bell chimed,
and a man stepped in —
mid-forties,
rumpled winter coat,
eyes dulled by the weight of routine.

He ordered a black coffee,
his voice low, almost mechanical.

As I poured his drink,
Karen rose and drifted to the counter,
her scarf trailing behind her.

"Would you like a cookie?" she asked.

He shook his head.
"Not much of a sweets person."

Karen smiled, unbothered.
"That's alright.
But there's one you might like."

She nodded toward the glass dome at the back.

He followed her gaze.
"That the one I've heard about?"

Karen didn't answer.
She simply looked at him —
a look that didn't search the surface,
but reached for the part he kept buried.

After a long pause, he sighed.
"Fine. Just to see what everyone's talking about."

She glanced at me,
and without a word, I knew to plate it.

He carried the cookie to a table near the window,
sat,
and after a beat, took a bite.

The shop faded.

He was in a dim hospital room,
seated at the bedside of his father.

The slow, steady beeping of the monitors filled the silence.

His father's eyes were closed,
breath shallow.

On the chair beside him rested a sealed envelope —
the last letter his father had written him.

In the vision, he picked it up,
opened it,
and felt the weight of words he'd avoided for years.

The shop returned.

His shoulders slumped,
his coffee untouched.

Karen was already standing just behind him.
She laid a gentle hand on his shoulder.

"Don't wait until silence has the last word."

His lips pressed together,
and he nodded once before rising quickly.

The bell above the door gave a softer chime
as he slipped out into the gray.

I turned to Karen.
"The moments we let slip by never return the same chance."

She didn't answer —
just placed her tin of cookies back on the table,
one hand resting on the lid
as if to keep the stars inside from scattering.

The Empty Stocking

A Simple Thank You

The week of Christmas always carried a strange hush in the
mornings, not from a lack of people,
but from the way the town itself seemed to slow.
Snow sat quietly on the awnings outside,
and the bells from the church down the street
marked the hour with a sound that felt older than the season.

I was once again refilling the pastry case
when a young man stepped in,
brushing snow off his hoodie.

Couldn't have been more than twenty, maybe twenty-one.

He had that half-grown confidence
of someone just figuring out who they were —
but with eyes that looked a little too tired for his age.

"Hot chocolate," he said. "Large."

He slid a few crumpled bills across the counter.

As I rang him up, his gaze wandered
to the small glass stand at the back.

"So… is that the thing?"

"What thing?" I asked.

"That cookie. My buddy said it… does something."

He shook his head in disbelief.

I lifted the dome.
"Some say it shows you what you need to see."

He shrugged, half skeptical.
"Alright. Why not."

He carried his drink and the cookie to a table near the window.

Outside, a kid in a bright red coat
was making snow angels in the little park across the street.

Inside, the young man broke the cookie in half
and took a bite.

The shop faded.

He was eight again,
standing in a dimly lit living room.

The tree was up,
but the bottom branches were bare —
no presents piled underneath,
just a single knitted stocking hanging from the mantel.

His parents were in the kitchen, talking quietly.
Money was tight.
Christmas that year had been… smaller.

He remembered feeling embarrassed back then —
thinking his friends would have stacks of gifts
while he had almost nothing to open.

But in the vision,
he saw something he hadn't seen before.

His mother was sitting at the kitchen table,
knitting late into the night,
the lamplight catching on her tired face.

She wasn't making a scarf to sell, or for herself —
she was knitting a pair of mittens to tuck into his stocking.

Sturdy, uneven, every stitch pulled tight with care.
It was all she could give,
and she'd poured every ounce of her love into the yarn.

Back in the shop, the young man blinked hard,
staring down at the half cookie left on the plate.

"I never… I never said thank you," his emotion now full.

Karen, who had been reading by the fire,
closed her book and spoke softly.

"It costs so little," she said.

He blinked, startled.
"What does?"

"To say it."
Her gaze flicked toward the empty stockings along the mantel.

He nodded, pulled out his phone,
and began typing a message.

His mouth lifted into a small, almost shy smile.
"She's gonna be shocked I even texted her before noon."

As he hurried to leave, he stopped, turned,
and walked back toward the counter.

In the most sincere way he was capable of in his newfound possibilities,
he said, "Thank you! I won't make that mistake again — not saying it
when I can."

I smiled and nodded.
"You are most welcome, young man.
It was absolutely my pleasure.
Merry Christmas!"

His smile brightened,
lighter than when he came in.

"And a Merry Christmas to you, as well!" as he shook my hand.

He left the other half of the cookie on the plate
and stepped out into the cold,
the bell above the door chiming in his wake.

And in that moment,
I realized: *sometimes the smallest gift can carry the biggest meaning.*

Julie's Meatloaf Dinner

Wrapped in Wax Paper

That night, the shop finally quieted after the dinner rush,
and I locked the door with that satisfying final click.
The air outside was crisp,
the snow squeaking under my boots on the walk home.
Inside, my little 1950s bungalow glowed like a Christmas card.

I'd spent years restoring it piece by piece —
refinishing the oak floors,
polishing the chrome handles on the cabinets,
painting the trim the same soft cream my mother used.

Stepping inside was like stepping back in time…
but in the best way.

The tree in the living room was already lit,
garland draped along the mantel,
candles glowing in the windows.

Boxes of outdoor lights waited in the corner
like unopened promises for another night.

I had just set a carton of ornaments on the coffee table
when the knock came.

Julie stepped in before I could even reach the door fully open,
brushing snow from her shoulders.

Ten years my senior,
she carried the same quick smile as Mom —
always made you feel like you'd just walked
into the best part of the day.

Tonight, she held a covered dish
that stopped me in my tracks.

"Brought you dinner," she said,
lifting the lid just enough for the aroma to escape.

"Mom's meatloaf.
Figured you could use the protein after all those cookies."

We set the table,
the tree lights casting a soft glow over the kitchen.

Between bites,
I hung a few ornaments
while Julie filled me in on town gossip —
her voice bouncing between teasing and genuine warmth.

"And what's this I hear about some secret cookie recipe?" she asked,
spearing a piece of meatloaf.

I laughed.
"Karen's doing.
I found it tucked away in an old notebook.
Not your average sugar cookie.
Let's just say… it's not about the taste."

She raised an eyebrow.
"You brought one home, didn't you?"

From the counter,
I lifted the small box I'd carried from the shop.

Inside, the golden cookie caught the lamplight.

I set it on a plate and slid it toward her.

"It's a choice," I said,
the same words I told my guests.

"But you won't know until you take a bite."

Julie looked from me to the cookie and back again,
then smirked.

"Well… little brother,
I've made riskier choices."

She broke it in half and took a bite.

The living room faded.

Her eyes softened almost immediately,
a slow breath leaving her
as if she'd just remembered something
she hadn't realized she'd forgotten.

I didn't ask. I knew better.

When she came back to herself,
she reached for her coffee, her voice quiet.

"She'd be so proud of you, you know.
For keeping the warmth going."

I swallowed the lump in my throat and nodded.
"That's the goal."

Julie carefully wrapped the other half of the cookie
in a square of wax paper,
folding it neat and precise —
just the way Mom used to wrap her holiday fudge.

Without a word, she slipped it into her bag,
carrying both the memory, and the promise forward.

James's First Journey

The Weight You Didn't Know You Carried

The morning after new snow had settled,
the shop felt like it had exhaled.
Yesterday's rush had given way to a softer rhythm —
where the old floorboards creaked
only if no one was talking.

I leaned against the counter,
cradling a heavy cream latte in both hands,
the warmth seeping deep into my palms.

Judy Garland's *Have Yourself a Merry Little Christmas*
threaded through the air —
not loud, but warm and close,
carrying both comfort and nostalgia.

I knew every note before it came.
Not because I'd played it a hundred times each December,
but because it lived in a place I visited often in my mind.

Karen was already there,
her scarf draped over the back of her chair,
a crossword puzzle angled just so.

She sipped her coffee
like she had all the time in the world,
her eyes lifting now and then
with that quiet awareness only she had.

The bell over the door opened
to a man in his late sixties.

Tall, still broad-shouldered,
though age had settled into him.

His winter coat looked like it had weathered many Decembers.

A familiar face —
a regular most of the year,
except around the holidays.

He hesitated at the threshold before stepping in.

Karen glanced up, studied him for a beat,
then returned to her puzzle,
humming softly along with the song.

"Morning, James," I said,
as if it were any other Tuesday.

He nodded, walked to the counter.
"Coffee. Black."

I poured and slid the mug toward him.

He held it in both hands but didn't drink.

His eyes drifted to the pastry case,
then to the small glass stand at the back.

"It's true, isn't it?"
His voice was low, gravelly.
"About that cookie."

Karen didn't look up,
but the faintest smile curved her lips once again.

I lifted the dome
and set one golden circle on a plate.

No garnish.
No flourish.
Just the shimmer of sugar under the lights.

James carried it to a corner table.

He broke the cookie in half,
took a bite,
and let his gaze fall —
not to the table,
but somewhere far beyond it.

His shoulders loosened.
His jaw unclenched.

The shop, the music, the morning —
all of it faded away for him.

When he returned,
his coffee was still hot.

His eyes were wet,
but his voice held steady.

"It was our first Christmas," he said quietly.
"Before the kids. Before the house.

She… she stayed up all night sewing me a necktie for work.
Said she couldn't afford to buy one.

I told her I didn't care about gifts."

He swallowed.
"I never noticed the blisters on her fingers until just now."

Karen closed her crossword.
"You noticed now," she said gently.

He nodded once.
"Yeah. I did." raising his eyebrows.

He stood, leaving the second half of the cookie untouched,
and tucked a bill under his cup.

At the door, he paused.

"Thank you," he said.

Then, after a beat:
"For the journey."

My eyes widened,
brows lifting at the words.

For the journey.

The phrase circled back,
landing with a weight I hadn't expected.

The bell chimed,
letting in the cold December air.

I turned to Karen.

She was already scribbling something
in the margin of her puzzle.

"Thoughts?" I asked.

Her eyes lifted, glinting.
"A moment to notice can carry a lifetime in the heart."

Margaret Lawson

Old Regrets, New Friends

Outside, the sidewalks bustled with shoppers,
scarves wrapped high,
laughter spilling into the cold air.
Inside, the shop hummed with low conversation,
the afternoon light slanting through the windows
just enough to turn the steam from the espresso machine
into ribbons of gold.

I was restocking the display case
when the bell above the door chimed
and in walked Margaret Lawson —
a name everyone in town knew.

Choir director for thirty years.
Keeper of tradition.

Her Christmas concerts were the kind
people rearranged their calendars for —
the paper covered it every December
with front-page photos:
Hometown Voices Shine Bright.

She didn't just enter a room —
she claimed it.

Deep red wool coat, buttoned to the neck.
Silk scarf perfectly draped.
Not a hair out of place.

She set her leather bag on the counter
as if it warranted its own chair.

But there was something in her eyes
I hadn't seen before —
a pause,
as if she'd stepped in from more than just the cold.

"Latte," she said.

Then, leaning in slightly:
"Extra hot.

And…" Her eyes flicked toward the back shelf.
"One of those." she commanded and pointed.

Karen, seated by the window
with her coffee and crossword,
didn't look up,
her smile unmistakable.

I poured the milk, watching the steam curl.
"You've heard about the cookie?"

Margaret's eyebrow arched.
"I've heard enough."

I set it before her.

She regarded the cookie
like she was about to audition it for a role,
then carried it to a table near the center of the room,
spine straight,
posture perfect.

She took a bite.

The shift in her eyes came almost instantly —
that flicker I'd learned to recognize
when someone's mind slipped out of the present.

She was nine again,
standing in the wings of the town hall auditorium.

The room warm with evergreen garlands
and the scent of wet wool coats drying from the snow.

She wore a white robe,
tinsel halo slightly crooked,
waiting to sing her solo in the Christmas pageant.

Her younger self stepped into the spotlight,
heart pounding,
voice steady.

The crowd leaned in.
She sang perfectly.

Applause washed over her like sunlight.

Then — a fragment she hadn't noticed before.

Off to the side,
a shy girl in the chorus stumbled over her line,
cheeks flushed.

Margaret remembered looking at her,
pride swelling,
and thinking:
She tried to ruin it.

But now she saw more.

Trembling hands.
Eyes searching for kindness,
finding none.

And herself — turning away.

Back in the shop,
she set the cookie down, breath catching.

Her shoulders sank, and she whispered, almost to herself:
"I chased the sound of my own voice,
and missed the harmony waiting beside it."

She looked my way for comfort, and ***this time*** my eyes returned it.
"Very poetic, as always, Margaret."

She gave a soft laugh, half self-conscious, half relieved.
"Maybe a little late, but I suppose better than never."

As she began to leave, my voice low
"Life may be a path of one, Maggie…
but it doesn't mean you have to ignore
the people walking beside you."

She was looking down as she heard it,
and a slight nod of affirmation slipped past her usual composure.
She gathered her things,
leaving the other half of the cookie on the plate —
not rejected,
but reserved,
as if waiting for someone else.

She left the shop the way she entered —
but less burdened, perhaps happier.

And as the door closed,
a curl of steam from the espresso machine
caught the light,
drifting after her like a ribbon of gold.

The Young Single Mom

Paper Chains

Snow tapped gently against the windows,
like it had nowhere else to be.
Inside, the fireplace crackled,
and the air was sweet with chocolate and espresso.
I was handing out samples of my mother's fudge recipe —
the one the town had come to love every year —
when she stepped in.

Mid-twenties,
a young single mother I'd seen before
but never without her little boy.

Today, she came alone.
Her hair was damp from the snow,
cheeks flushed,
eyes carrying a list she couldn't seem to set down.

"Coffee, please," she said,
brushing a strand of hair behind her ear.
"Extra cream."

Karen sat at her usual table by the window,
crossword folded beside her,
sipping her coffee as if the only appointment she had that day
was watching snow fall.

When the young woman's gaze drifted to the pastry case,
it caught on the glass stand at the back.

"So, there it is!" she said, not looking away.

I set down her coffee.
"Indeed. May I interest you in one?"
I said with a half-smile.

She hesitated, then nodded.
I placed the cookie on a plate,
the sugar crystals catching the warm shop light.

She carried it to a table,
sat,
and just looked at it —
as though she needed assurance it was allowed to bring her comfort.

Then she broke it in half,
lifted one piece,
and took a bite.

The shop faded.

She was eight again,
cross-legged on the living-room carpet.

In the kitchen,
her parents' voices were sharp,
arguing about money —
about how Christmas was going to look
without the usual pile of gifts.

She glanced at the tree,
bare beneath
except for the paper chain she'd been making for weeks.

Bright loops of red and green construction paper,
each link carefully glued and pressed.

Her small hands worked quietly,
snipping and looping,
as if the chain itself could hold the season together.

When her mother finally came in
and sat beside her —
the argument still clinging to her eyes —
she didn't mention the missing presents.

She just picked up the scissors
and joined in,
making link after link,
humming softly with the radio.

And somehow, in that moment —
paper chains, lamplight,
her mother's quiet presence —
the world felt whole.

Back in the shop,
she set down the other half of the cookie,
gaze lingering somewhere between here and there.

"I've been killing myself
trying to make Christmas perfect for my son," she whispered.
"And all he's ever really needed… is me?" as she looked my way.

"Memories last longer
than anything you could buy," I noted.

The woman smiled —
small, but real —
and wrapped her hands around her mug
as if to hold on to the thought.

At the door, she paused, glanced back.
A silent *thank you* formed on her lips.
I nodded as she left the shop.

I thought about the chains we carry —
some forged heavy like Marley's,
others looped together out of love.

Both endure.
One weighs us down.
The other sets us free.

Outside, the snow tapped at the windows —
patient, steady,
as if it already understood the worth
of simply being near.

Peter and the Missing Cinnamon Roll

Sometimes the loss is the point

The bell chimed and Peter ducked in,
stamping snow from his boots,
cheeks red from the cold.

"You're out of cinnamon rolls already?"
he said, as though I'd personally betrayed him.

"It's eleven a.m., Peter.
You snooze, you lose."

We both laughed.

He ordered a coffee,
leaning an elbow on the counter.

"Good. Cinnamon rolls are a gateway drug.
I'm trying to keep my options open…
in pastry and in love."

Karen, at her usual table,
didn't even look up from her crossword.

"Maybe pick one to focus on.
You might have better luck."

Peter grinned.
"Karen, you're my idol.
When I grow up,
I want your level of confidence."

Karen's pen didn't pause.
"Confidence comes from knowing what you want.
Growing up is optional."

She punctuated it with a quick wink.

Peter chuckled, shaking his head.
"Maybe that's why I'm always late —
for the cinnamon rolls,
and everything else worth having."

He laughed,
raised his cup in a mock toast,
and headed out.

The bell above the door chimed once more.

Ryan Bennett

It's not always the other person

The Saturday before Christmas
always carried a strange energy —
half excitement,
half exhaustion.

Outside, bundled shoppers wove through market stalls,
carolers harmonies soothing the frosted air.

Inside, the shop hummed with conversation,
the warmth of sugar, cinnamon,
and melting snow.

I was tamping espresso for a heavy cream latte
when the door swung open
and in came Ryan Bennett.

Mid-forties, tailored coat,
hair just a little too perfect.

He wore the kind of smile
a man keeps after years
of being told he's charming —
wins a room
while still holding it at arm's length.

"Greg!" he said like we were old friends,
though we'd only met twice.

"Full house in here today.
You must be killing it."

Karen glanced up from her crossword by the window.
Her eyes lingered, then returned to the page.

"Keeping busy," I said evenly.
"What'll it be?"

"Americano. And…"

His gaze drifted to the back shelf,
where the glass dome sat glowing in the shop light.

"That cookie everyone whispers about.
People say it's 'magic'?"

I lifted the dome.
"Some say that, huh?"

He smirked.
"Well, I've had a hell of a year.
The universe owes me a win."

Karen's pen paused mid-word.
She didn't look up,
but the faint shake of her head said enough.

I placed the cookie before him.
"Enjoy."

He sat near the door and — without ceremony —
bit into it.

The shop faded.

He was nineteen again,
hunched in a diner booth across from his first girlfriend.

Christmas lights blinked weakly in the window,
the smell of fries and cocoa thick in the air.

"Ryan… I feel like you're pulling away,"
she said softly.

He remembered his laugh —
sharp, dismissive.

"You're imagining things."

Now he saw what he hadn't then:
the slump of her shoulders,
the hurt in her eyes before she masked it
with a brittle smile.

He saw how he'd flipped the night into a debate
about her flaws,
forcing her to carry the blame
he refused to claim.

Then the flashes came —
woman after woman,
the same script,
the same escape.

Always the hero of his own tragedy.

Back in the shop,
Ryan lowered the cookie,
smirk gone.

"Guess it's not always the other person,"
he said quietly.

I nodded.
"It's always about us.
Never about them."

Karen closed her crossword
and looked straight at him.

"The hardest stories to rewrite," she said gently,
"are the ones we've told ourselves for the longest time."

Ryan gave a short, humorless laugh.
"Yeah. Guess I've got some *editing* to do."

He left the Americano untouched,
the bell over the door chiming him into the cold.

Karen shook her head.
"Some people think the cookie owes them something.

It's just reflecting
the pattern of their own choices."

I glanced at the untouched coffee,
the plate with a half-eaten cookie.

"Sooner or later, the past stops being a story —
and starts becoming a mirror."

Peter's Comfort Drink

A Warm Cup for a Cold Truth

I was wiping down the counter
when Peter wandered in,
scarf half-on,
hair windblown
like he'd left the house mid-thought.

"Hot chocolate," he said.
"It's a comfort drink day."

I poured it, raising an eyebrow.
"That bad?"

He sighed.
"Another romance bites the dust.
She just didn't get me."

Karen glanced over the top of her book.
"Or you didn't get her."

She took a slow sip,
then added with a chuckle,
"You were late for the cinnamon rolls too, Peter.
Some habits run deep."

Peter pointed at her
like she'd just scored the winning point.

"See, Greg? This is why Karen
is the oracle of our neighborhood —
brutal honesty wrapped in charm."

I slid the hot chocolate across to him.
"You ever think maybe the common factor

in all these stories…
is you?"

He smirked.
"You sound like my sister…
and my last therapist."

The smirk lingered for a beat,
then faltered,
just enough to let a shadow through.

He left with the drink,
the steam curling into the cold air
as the bell chimed him out —

and a faint crease between his brows
that said he'd heard more
than he wanted to admit.

Warm Bread from the Oven

Finding What Nourishes You

The shop was steady this morning,
the hum of voices rising and falling
with the bustle of the holiday.

Karen sat in her usual seat,
coffee cooling beside her,
eyes fixed on the snowfall.

The bell chimed,
and a man in his early sixties stepped in.
Well-dressed, but with the tired look
of someone carrying a personal burden.

He ordered chamomile tea — nothing else.

As I prepared it,
his gaze flicked toward the glass dome on the back shelf.
"That's the famous cookie, right?"

"Indeed," I replied with a smile.

He nodded absently,
carried his tea to a small table in the corner.
Twice, maybe three times,
I caught him glancing toward the cookie —
but he didn't ask.

Karen never turned,
but in the window's reflection,
I caught her eyes on him.

Minutes passed.
He sipped, checked his watch, sighed.

Finally, almost reluctantly,
he returned to the counter.
"Alright… give me one."

I plated it and set it down.
He carried it back,
steam curling from his tea
as if the warmth itself had been waiting for him.

He broke off a piece,
paused,
then dipped it gently into his cup.

The shop faded.

He was home again on Christmas Eve,
the house alive with pine and baking bread.
His mother was in the kitchen,
calling him in to help.

He remembered brushing her off,
too absorbed in his new toy train.
She only smiled,
kneading quietly,
wanting nothing more than his company.

Back in the shop,
his hand lingered on the table
before reaching for his phone.

Karen still hadn't turned toward him.
But as he rose to leave, she spoke to the glass.

"Doesn't bread taste best
when it's still warm?"

He stopped,
just for a moment,

then smiled faintly
and stepped into the snow.

She lifted her cup,
eyes still on the window.

"Sometimes," she paused,
"I think about my mother pulling warm bread from the oven. The smell filled the whole house — it was enough to make me feel safe, even before a word was spoken."
She looked back at me, eyes soft.

And in that moment, I realized Karen's story
reached far deeper than she ever let on.

James's Second Journey

The gift, the moment, and the vow not to miss it again

The shoppe was busier
than a Tuesday had any right to be.
Snow fell soft outside —
making people linger over their coffee longer
instead of rushing back to their errands.

The air carried that low holiday murmur,
voices blending with the hiss of the espresso machine.

I was topping off the chocolate chip jar
when the bell chimed
and in walked James.

Same weathered coat,
same steady gait,
but something different in his face —
like he'd been rehearsing a line on the way over.

Karen was by the window,
a book open in front of her.
She looked up when she saw him,
her gaze holding a beat too long
before she lowered it back to the page.

"Morning, James," I said.
"Back so soon?"

He came to the counter,
eyes flicking toward the glass dome.
"If it's alright…
I'll take another."

I raised an eyebrow.
"Second journeys can be… different."

"That's what I'm hoping for," he said softly.
"The first one… it stayed with me."

I nodded,
slid a cookie onto a plate,
and set it before him.

He carried it to the same corner table.
For a moment, he only sat there,
fingers resting on the rim of the plate —
like he was bracing himself
for wherever it might take him.

Then he took a bite.

The shop faded.

This time he wasn't in the quiet glow
of his first Christmas with his wife.

He was in a hospital room, years later.
Sterile air tinged with antiseptic.
The steady pulse of monitors filling the silence.

She was in the bed,
pale but smiling,
her hand resting in his.

Beside him sat a poorly wrapped package —
a book of poems she'd loved since college.

He saw himself then:
weary, distracted,
nodding politely as she handed it to him.
Setting it aside

because the nurse had come in with her medication.
Telling himself he'd read it later.

He never had.

In the vision,
he picked it up, opened it,
and began to read aloud.

Her breathing slowed,
her eyes closing — not from fatigue, but from peace.

It wasn't the poems that mattered.
It was his presence.

Back in the shop,
James wiped his eyes
and exhaled long.

"The first cookie…
it took me to the beginning.
This one… to the end.

I missed it twice —
the gift, the moment… both times."

Karen closed her book,
voice low but clear.

"And now you've seen it twice.
The question is —
will you miss it a third time?"

James nodded slowly,
as if making a vow only he could hear.

He stood,
left half the cookie untouched,

and pressed a hand to my shoulder
before stepping into the snow.

Karen didn't look up.
She sipped her coffee and murmured,

"Life is short.
when it whispers to you, it's always best to listen."

Marcus Davis

The Door You Chose

The late afternoon sun
painted the shoppe in amber light.
Snowflakes drifted past the windows.
From the stereo,
Peggy Lee's Christmas Waltz celebrated the holidays.
Karen sat in her usual spot,
book open but unread.

The bell chimed,
and in stepped Marcus Davis.

Early thirties.
Broad-shouldered.
Still carrying the easy athleticism
of a man who once had the world at his feet.
A local boy turned college football star —
until a knee injury ended any shot at the NFL.

Around town,
he was known for coaching youth sports
and working the family construction business.

But when Marcus spoke of life,
it was always divided into
before the injury
and after the injury.

"Greg," he said with a nod,
peeling off his gloves.
"Hot mocha. Extra whip."

I started on his drink.
"You've got the look of a man
killing time before something important."

He smirked.
"Not much important these days."

Karen looked at him over her glasses, smiling,
"That's not the same as nothing important."

Marcus gave a polite chuckle
that didn't touch his eyes.

His gaze shifted to the glass dome on the back shelf.
"That the cookie everyone talks about?"

I lifted the lid,
set one on a plate.
"The one and only."

He studied it,
then took a decisive bite.

The shop faded.

He was back in the locker room at twenty-one,
the sting of sweat and winter air
mixing with the metallic tang of weight benches.
His knee was wrapped in ice.

The game had ended hours ago — his game, his season, his shot.

This time, he saw what he hadn't then:
his coach kneeling beside him,
saying leadership wasn't just about playing —
it was about showing up in a different way now.

Marcus nodded,
but his mind was already pulling away,
lost in what he thought life owed him.

The vision shifted.

A youth football field, present day.
Kids running drills in mismatched gear,
breath puffing in the cold.
One boy fell hard and stayed down.

Marcus jogged over,
offered a hand,
said something that made the boy
square his shoulders and rise taller.
The boy's grin said it all.

The air carried the same winter bite
as that locker room years ago —
but this time, the cold carried laughter, not silence.

Back in the shop,
Marcus stared at the half-eaten cookie.

"I've been stuck," he said.
"Always looking back at the door that closed.
Never noticed the one open right in front of me."

Karen closed her book.
"Doors don't close and open, Marcus.
They're all open.
We just choose which ones to walk through."

A faint smile touched his lips.
He picked up the other half of the cookie
and carried it with him toward the door.

"My field is still *wide* open."

The bell chimed behind him.

Karen's reflection in the window
wore the same knowing smile as the first day.

"You can't know where you're going," she said softly,
"if you don't know what you're already doing."

The song swelled —
Peggy Lee's voice lilting through the shop,
smooth and warm as the amber light.

David Cole

Baking Can Be the Sweetest Gift

The late afternoon light streamed through the windows,
turning the snow into something staged —
a set built for memory.
Inside, the air was heavy with the scent of my mother's bishop's bread,
fresh from the oven,
warmth layered into the walls.

Karen sat at her table,
not with a book this time,
but folding a napkin into the shape of a star,
her fingers moving with quiet precision.

The bell chimed,
and in walked David Cole.
Early fifties.
Polished.
Carried himself like time bent to his schedule.

He owned half of Main Street,
and had opinions on the rest.

"Cappuccino," he said,
leaning on the counter
with the ease of someone used to being agreed with.

His gaze drifted toward the glass dome.
"Ah… the cookie.
I've heard the stories.
People say it changes them."

"It doesn't change you," I said.
"It shows you."

David smirked.
"Shows me what?"

"Whatever you've been avoiding."

He gave a dry chuckle.
"I've faced harder truths than a cookie can offer."

I slid the plate across.
"It's your choice.
But once you take a bite,
you don't get to choose what you see."

He carried it to a table near Karen's.
One bite —
chewed slowly,
like he was testing the legend.

And then his gaze stilled.

The shop faded.

He was back in his office,
ten years earlier.
The radiator rattled against the December chill.
On his desk sat a small tin,
the scent of butter and sugar still rising from it.

His assistant —
young, nervous,
eager —
stood waiting as he lifted the lid.

Inside, rows of cookies,
neatly wrapped in wax paper.
Her grandmother's Christmas recipes.

"Thought you might like some," she said softly.
"I bake them every year."

He remembered barely glancing up,
already reaching for a file.
"Thanks," he muttered.

She lingered —
just a moment —
waiting for something more.
Then left quietly.

And one by one,
faces followed —
different assistants,
different offerings,
different gestures of simple humanity
he had never received,
never let matter.

Dismissed with nods,
shrugged into silence,
until the truth stood there in front of him:
he hadn't built an empire alone.
He'd just never noticed
the hands that steadied the walls.

The shop returned.

Karen didn't look up from her folded star.
"You've got more than property to manage, David."

For once,
the smirk was gone.

He rose,
paused at the counter.

"What was in that case again?" he asked,
gesturing toward the shelves behind me.

"Family recipes," I said.
"Chocolate chip,
icebox,
minty jewels,
brownie drops…
plus bishop's bread, fudge,
and Mom's bon bons."

David gave a slow nod.
"Greg…
box me up a dozen of your family's recipes,
all of it.

This time,
I'd like to give the right gift."

I packed the box carefully,
slid it across.
He held it a moment,
as if feeling the weight of what it carried.

"Feels lighter than it should," he said quietly,
"but heavier than it looks."

Peter's Bro Hug

The first bite is to see it. The second is to own it

The afternoon snow outside looked half-hearted —
flurries drifting lazily down,
melting as soon as they touched the pavement.
Inside, the shop hummed
with that low warmth of conversation.

The bell chimed,
and Peter stepped in, brushing snow from his jacket.
He spotted me behind the counter and grinned.

"Greg, I'm retiring from dating apps.
My heart can't take another profile picture
with a hidden boyfriend lurking in the background."

I chuckled.
"You've said that before."

"This time, I mean it," he said, dropping onto a stool.
"Coffee. Black.
And—" his glance flicked to the glass dome,
"—is that… *the one*?"

He didn't have to name *The Christmas Cookie.*

I lifted the dome.
"It doesn't fix anything.
It just shows what you need to see."

Peter smirked.
"Fine.
Show me."
I plated it.
He took a bite.

The shop faded.

He was twenty-seven again,
in a crowded bar,
the air thick with beer and fried food.

Across from him sat Anna — the one who got away.
She was telling him they weren't a match,
her voice calm but sure.

He remembered arguing,
poking holes in her reasons,
turning goodbye into a debate.

This time he saw what he'd missed:
the quiet sadness in her eyes,
the way she was trying to leave him with dignity.

The scenes blurred —
other women, other moments —
the same script playing out again and again.

Always making the other person wrong
so he wouldn't have to look at himself.

Back in the shop,
Peter stared at the cookie, his jaw tight.

"Guess I've been… *consistent*, you might say" he said.

"Patterns aren't curses, Peter.
They're choices you keep making."

He gave a short laugh, more sigh than humor.
"Yeah. Well… guess I know my New Year's resolution."

He pushed the plate away,
the second half untouched.

"I'm not ready for the rest yet."

As he stood, I handed him his coat.
"You don't have to make others wrong
when others are doing something right for themselves."

He reached for my hand,
then pulled me into the "bro hug" —
that hug built over the years of assurance,
and the quiet certainty
that a true friend will watch your back,
bring you honesty,
even when you least expect it.

His voice caught as he said,
"I truly appreciate your kindness and friendship all these years, my man."

He lingered for another moment,
catching his emotion.
He turned and left without looking back.

Karen's voice followed him softly:
"The first bite is to see it.
The second is to own it."

I watched my friend disappear into the snow,
the warmth of the shop at my back,
hoping this time, the truth would follow him home.

The Young Woman Who Closed the Door

Sometimes the end is the beginning

The snow outside looked like it was holding its breath —
waiting, suspended —
and inside, the shop mirrored it.

The fire crackled low,
and the only music was the soft jazz of White Christmas,
quiet enough
that even silence seemed part of the arrangement.

A young woman stepped in, mid-twenties maybe,
her coat dusted with snow.
She moved like someone carrying a weight you couldn't see.
Her eyes flicked toward the glass dome almost immediately,
as though she already knew why she was here.

"Latte," she said softly,
"and… the cookie."

I made her drink,
placed the cookie on a plate,
and set it in front of her.

"It's a choice," I said.

She gave a small nod
and carried it to a table near the fire.

She took a sip of her latte,
then broke the cookie in half
and took a bite.

The shop faded for her.

But this time,
I felt another gaze.

Karen wasn't watching the woman at all.
She was watching me —
steady, unblinking,
as if she knew this one wasn't hers to witness.

The young woman was sitting on the floor of a dimly lit bedroom;
Christmas lights strung across the wall.
She was packing a duffel bag.

In the corner, a man's voice was raised —
sharp, cutting.

She was leaving,
but the shame in her eyes
wasn't about what had been done to her.
It was about the years she'd spent
convincing herself she deserved it.
That she had to endure it.

Now, with the zipper's tug,
she was rewriting that story.

In the vision,
she zipped the bag, stood,
and walked out the door into the cold night.
She didn't look back.

Back in the shop,
she placed the half cookie down carefully,
almost like she didn't want to disturb it.

Karen spoke before I could.
"The greatest gift closure can give back… is you."

The young woman looked at her and nodded,
eyes shining.
"Yeah," she whispered.
"Yeah, it is."

She left quietly,
the bell above the door giving its small, warm note.

I turned to Karen.
"You weren't even watching her."

Karen held my gaze a moment longer than I expected.
"I didn't need to."

She took a sip of her coffee.
"You did."

Sometimes the end really is the beginning.

Karen hadn't needed to see her journey —
I had.

And I had.

Greg's Bite

Your Own Journey Waits For No One

The shop had just closed for the night.
Snow continued outside.

Chairs were turned upside down on tables,
the fire had burned to embers,
and the only light came from the strings
draped along the windows.

I was wiping down the counter
when my eyes drifted to the glass dome.
The cookie sat centered,
its sugar crystals catching the glow like frost.

I paused.

For weeks, I'd watched people take the bite —
the gasps, the tears, the small, quiet smiles.
I'd seen the way it stripped away pretense,
how it cut straight to something
you couldn't hide from.

And I'd always been the one on the outside,
holding the plate,
watching it happen.

I lifted the dome.

The smell was warm and faintly sweet,
but what I felt wasn't hunger.
It was a pull.
Not from the cookie itself,
but from the question it carried.

What would it show me?

Karen's voice broke the silence.
"That's not the question to ask yourself."

I hadn't heard her come up.
She was standing just inside
the glow of the window lights,
coffee cup in hand.

I set the dome back down.
"Then what is?"

Her eyes didn't waver.
"It's not what it would show you.
It's whether you're willing to see it."

I let out a small laugh,
but it didn't feel like humor.
"And you think I'm not?"

She tilted her head.
"I think everyone believes they are —
until the moment arrives."

We stood in the hush for a beat,
the wind pressing softly against the windows.

Then she turned toward the door,
her voice trailing back:

"Close up, Gregory.
The cookie isn't going anywhere."

The bell gave its faintest chime as she left.

I looked again at the cookie under glass,
its sugar glittering in the low light.

I didn't reach for it.
And maybe that was the loudest choice of all.

I turned off the lights
and headed home.

James's Journey Home

Some journeys only need to be taken once

The shop had been steady all morning,
the fire working hard against the draft at the door.
I was restocking the icebox cookie jar
when the bell chimed.
It was James.

Same weathered coat,
same steady walk —
but unmistakably different.
His shoulders sat lighter,
the lines at his eyes eased.
Even his gait carried a quiet ease.

Karen looked up from her coffee.
Not at him — at me.

"Greg," James said warmly,
"thought I'd stop in for one of those lattes of yours.
Extra hot, like last time."

I smiled.
"You're looking… different."

He chuckled.
"Feels different.
Went and visited the spot where I first met my wife.
Sat there for hours.
I don't know if it's closure or something else,
but I left feeling lighter.
Guess I finally caught up to what that cookie showed me."

Karen took a slow sip, still watching me.
I handed him his latte. "Glad to hear it."

He lingered,
then glanced toward the glass dome.
"Not here for the cookie today.
Some things, you only need to see once.
I guess in my case, twice."

As he left, he placed a small book on the counter.
"Thought you might like this. Poems.
The same book my wife gave me.
Figured someone should read it."
The bell above the door
gave a softer chime than usual.

I stood holding the book,
its worn cover breathing with memory
beneath my fingertips.

Karen's voice broke the quiet. "You see it?"

I looked at her. "See what?"

She tilted her head slightly.
"The way he walked in here the first time…
and the way he just walked out."

Her gaze didn't waver.

"It was never about the cookie, Gregory.
It's about the letting go."

For a second, I wasn't sure if she was still talking about James.

Not Today, Gregory

Some Visions Aren't Made For Today

The snow outside was falling
in fat, lazy flakes —
casting a hush across the street.

Inside, the fire burned steady,
and the scent of cinnamon rolls lingered in the air
like memory itself.

Karen sat in her usual spot,
glasses low on her nose,
her book closed.
She was waiting.

The bell chimed,
and a man about my age stepped in.

His coat was dusted with snow,
scarf loose,
eyes tired but searching.

He ordered a heavy cream latte —
extra hot.

That caught my attention.

As I made it,
his gaze drifted to the glass dome.
"That the one?"

I nodded.
"That's the one."

He hesitated,
then said quietly,
"Yeah… I'll take it."

He carried the plate to a table by the fire,
sat,
and after a long breath,
took a bite.

The shop faded for him.

And this time,
I felt it too —
as if I was standing just behind his shoulder
inside the vision.

A warm kitchen.
Popcorn and cranberry garland
strung across the windows.
A radio in the corner,
crackling through *Silver Bells*.

His mother bent over a tray of rolls,
her hair caught in a red scarf.
She looked back at him,
smiling with a tenderness
that was theirs alone.

Then the kitchen was empty.
The rolls cooling.
The radio silent.

My fingers gripped the counter,
knuckles white.
My own memory stirred —
not the same,
but close enough to ache.

I took a step toward the dome.

Karen's voice cut the hush.
"Not today, Gregory."

I froze.
"What—?"

She shook her head gently,
not unkind.

"You're not ready yet."

The man finished his latte
and slipped out quietly,
the bell above the door
giving its small, sorrowful chime.

The ache in my chest remained.

The Last Nudge

A reminder that even you belong in the story

It was late evening.
The shop was closed, chairs up, lights low.
The only illumination came from the fire,
throwing soft shadows across the counter.

Outside, the street was nearly empty,
snow piled high along the edges.

I was wiping down the espresso machine
when the bell above the door chimed.

It was Karen.
She never came in after closing.

She walked straight to her table,
set down her coat,
and without a word, went to the counter.

From her bag,
she pulled a small tin
and placed it beside the glass dome.

Inside were star-shaped cookies —
the same ones she'd given away weeks ago.

"I thought we were done for the day," I said.
"We are," she replied,
taking a seat at the counter instead of her usual table.

She opened the tin,
slid it toward me.
"These aren't for customers.
They're for you."

I glanced at the glass dome.
"And that?"

She followed my gaze.
"That's still for you too.
You just haven't decided to take it."

I gave a short laugh.
"You've been trying to get me to eat that cookie all along, haven't you?"

Karen didn't smile.
"Gregory… everyone comes into this shop for a reason.
Even you."

Something in her voice made me still.

I looked at the cookie under the dome —
its sugar catching the firelight,
looking almost alive.

"What if I'm not ready?"

Her eyes didn't waver.
"Then wait.
But don't confuse waiting with living."

We sat in silence.
The fire popped.
The clock above the door ticked toward the hour.

Before she left,
she placed her hand lightly on my arm.

"When you're ready," she said softly,
"don't think.
Just bite."

She smiled,
squeezed my arm, gave a wink,
and walked to the door.

The bell chimed as she stepped out into the night,
leaving me alone with the cookie.

The shop was hushed —
the kind of quiet that makes you aware of your own breathing.
Outside, snow blurred the streetlamps into soft halos.

I was halfway through wiping the counter
when my eyes landed on the glass dome.
The cookie sat there,
unassuming as ever —
to change dozens of lives this month.
Including mine.

I'd been avoiding this.
Not because I didn't want to see,
but because I wasn't sure I could bear
what I might see differently this time.

The first bite had left me rattled —
a memory I'd sidestepped for years,
dropped in my lap without warning.
Regret still clung to it,
heavy as wet wool.

But tonight felt different.
Maybe it was everything I'd witnessed this season —
the way people returned from their journeys softer, more certain.
Or maybe it was knowing Julie
still had her own second half waiting.

Either way, I lifted the dome.

The scent hit first —
butter and spice,
warm and familiar.

This time I didn't rush.
I poured a coffee,
set it beside the plate,
and took a seat at the counter.

The first bite was familiar.
Soft. Rich.
And then came the pull —
that warm current tugging me out of the room,
out of myself.

And suddenly, I was there.

On that street.
That day.
The conversation I'd dreaded replaying
in perfect clarity.

Only… I wasn't the same man watching.
This time, I didn't just see what I'd done wrong.
I saw why I'd done it.
The fear that drove the choice.
The version of me that didn't yet know
how to stand still in discomfort.

For the first time,
I felt compassion for him —
for me —
in a way I couldn't before.

And in that compassion,
the scene loosened its grip.
Still a moment I'd never undo.

But no longer a chain around my neck.
Now it was a mile marker —
proof of distance traveled.

When I blinked,
I was back in the shop.
The coffee was still hot.
Half a cookie sat on the plate.

I smiled.
the epiphany whispered,
and for once,
I was listening.

I wrapped the second half in wax paper.

I wrapped the second half in wax paper.
Julie's name was already in my mind
when I found myself standing outside her little craftsman-style home,
its windows glowing warm against the snow.

Julie met me at the door with a smile
that was more knowing than casual.
"Soup's hot.
Bread's almost done," she said,
stepping back to let me in.

After we ate,
she went to the mantel,
picked up a small tin,
and set it between us.

"I've been saving something," she said,
lifting the lid.
Inside, wrapped neatly in wax paper,

was the second half of the cookie
she'd bitten weeks ago at my place.

She unwrapped it slowly,
as if it might shatter.

"I wasn't sure when I'd be ready," she admitted.
"But tonight felt like the night."

She took the bite.
Her eyes went distant,
hands resting in her lap.

I didn't speak.
I'd learned these moments belonged entirely
to the one taking the journey.

I couldn't see what she saw,
but when she returned,
there was a softness in her expression
I hadn't seen in years.

"Greg," she said quietly,
"I saw Christmas morning, 1969.
You were six.
I'd just turned sixteen.
Mom was still in her robe,
trying to keep you from eating half the cinnamon rolls
before they cooled.

You were so excited
you didn't notice she'd been up all night
wrapping your presents
so you wouldn't wake to an empty tree."

Her voice caught.
"I saw her hands…

I'd forgotten how young they were.
How strong."

Finally she smiled,
small and steady.
"I think I understand now
why you guard that cookie the way you do."

We sat in the hush of it,
the fire soft behind us,
when Julie suddenly laughed,
shaking her head.

"The strangest thing happened today.
David Cole stopped by the house.
I guess he thought Katelyn still lived here.
Dropped off a tin of cookies for her —
told me to wish her Merry Christmas.

He didn't even realize you and I were related.
Didn't know I'd recognize the recipes
came straight from Mom."

Her eyes glinted with amusement.
"Imagine that.
Your shop's cookies
making their way back home."

The snow was still falling
when I left later that night.
The cold nipped at my face,
but beneath it
I could almost swear I caught
the faint, warm scent of cinnamon rolls on the air —
as if her memory had slipped outside with me.

Walking home,
I thought about how one bite
had tied us both
to the same pair of hands…
two different memories,
woven by the same thread of love.

And maybe that was the real magic —
not the cookie itself,
but the way it carried her back to the beginning,
and let me forgive myself for mine.

The Art of Noticing

Listening for the part they're not speaking out loud

The shop was nearly empty.
Outside, the snow had stopped,
leaving a white stillness
that made the world feel paused.
Inside, the only sounds were the low crackle of the fire,
and the faint clink of my spoon against a mug
as I stirred my latte.

Karen sat nearer the counter than usual,
as if the day had nudged her closer.
No book. No crossword. No knitting.
Just her hands wrapped around her coffee,
her gaze fixed on somewhere I couldn't see.

I carried my cup over and sat across from her.
"You always seem to know," I said.

Her eyes returned slowly,
like they were adjusting to this world again.
She gave a gentle smile.
"Know what?"

"What people need," I said.
"It's not like you ask questions.
You just… land on the thing that matters most."

The faintest smile brushed her face.
"It's not about knowing, Greg.
It's about noticing."

I tilted my head.
"Noticing?"

She lifted a shoulder, almost casual.
"The way someone grips a cup.
How their eyes flick when they think no one's looking.
The pause before they answer something simple.
Most people are already telling you what they need —
they just don't know it."

I leaned back, sipping slowly.
"So you listen."

Karen's gaze held mine,
steady enough that I felt it in my chest.
"I listen for the part they're not speaking out loud.
I listen for what's being said in their actions."

The words settled between us,
warm as the fire's glow

After a while I asked,
"And the cookie?"

Her smile deepened — quiet, certain.
"The cookie just makes it harder to ignore
what they've been whispering to themselves all along."

We let the silence stretch,
the fire popping softly.

And in that pause,
I realized even the smallest things —
the hush of the snow outside,
the faint sweetness still lingering in the air —
were telling their own story.

You just had to notice.

And suddenly,
I wondered how many things in my own life
had been there all along,
waiting for me to finally notice.

The Counter on Christmas Eve

The Warmth of Family, The Glow of the Season

The shop was hushed — as if the whole world held its breath..
Outside, snow fell in soft waves, catching the streetlamps,
tumbling in slow-motion halos.
Inside, the fire burned low,
and the scent of Mom's cookies and coffee wrapped itself around the room like a blanket.

The glass dome sat on the counter, as always —
but tonight, I didn't see it as a thing to resist or fear.
Tonight, it felt like a promise.

Karen came in later than usual,
her scarf trailing, a dusting of snow in her hair.
She ordered her coffee, extra hot,
and took her place by the window.

We didn't speak at first.
The silence was companionable — threaded with all we'd already shared.

At last, she glanced up from her book.
"It's different, isn't it?"

I nodded.
"Everything's the same… and nothing is the same."

A faint smile curved her mouth.
"That's how you know you saw what you were meant to see."

Before I could answer, the bell chimed again.
Julie stepped inside, cheeks bright from the cold,
carrying a small tin in one hand
and a single star ornament in the other.

"Merry Christmas, little brother," she said —
the same words she'd spoken every year of my life —
as she set the ornament on the counter.

She slid onto the stool beside me,
leaning toward Karen to whisper something
that made Karen laugh —
an easy laugh that softened her whole face.

Without hesitation, Karen left her table
and joined us at the counter.
The three of us sat shoulder to shoulder,
steam rising from our mugs
as the first notes of *Have Yourself a Merry Little Christmas*
drifted from the old stereo in the corner.

The music wrapped around us,
the conversation folding into easy laughter.

And in the middle of it, I noticed our hands —
Julie's resting on the counter,
mine around my mug,
Karen's reaching for her cup.

All the hands the cookie had connected this season.
Some here.
Some far away.
Some gone — never really gone.

If this were a Christmas movie, the camera would slowly pull back:
the glow of the shop spilling onto the snow-covered street,
the three of us framed in that circle of light.

Outside, the snow fell heavier,
blanketing the quiet town.
And inside, at that counter on Christmas Eve,

none of us carried anything
we weren't willing to take with us into the morning.

For once, the night asked for nothing more.

I never asked Karen how she always knew.
Some things, I think, aren't meant to be explained.

But once, long after closing,
I found a folded slip of paper tucked under the glass dome.
It wasn't signed.
Just three words, written in a hand I
instantly recognized:

I've taken mine.

Not every story ends with answers.
Some end with memories —
the kind that follow you home,
season after season,
and every Christmas thereafter.

And that is enough.

Epilogue

The bell knows every story

Snow drifts against the windows of Brookhaven Pines,
steady as breath.
Inside, the warmth held.
The fire hummed.
The cookie waited beneath its glass dome.

And when the bell above the door rang once more,
the shop exhaled —
ready for the next story,
the next journey,
the next choice.

A Note from the Author

Stories are never just words on a page.
They're memory, laughter, ache, and hope,
gathered together like recipes passed down
through hands that cared enough to write them.

This book began at the counter of a small shop in my imagination —
but maybe you felt echoes of your own life in its pages.
A pattern you've known.
A moment you've longed to revisit.
A reminder that your own story is still being written,
choice by choice.

The Christmas Cookie
was never about magic sugar or flour.
It was always about the heartbeat beneath —
the truth that when we notice,
when we choose,
when we let go,
we carry ourselves forward
lighter than before.

So thank you for sitting at the counter with me,
for sharing a cup of coffee,
for taking a bite of the story.
May the warmth you found here
follow you home,
season after season,
and every Christmas thereafter.

With gratitude,
David Gregory

www.ingramcontent.com/pod-product-compliance
Lightning Source LLC
Chambersburg PA
CBHW070620310726
48982CB00001B/132

* 9 7 9 8 9 9 9 9 0 2 1 1 *